THE QUEEN OF THE FROGS

Written by Davide Cali
Illustrated by Marco Somà

Translated by
Lyn Miller-Lachmann

Eerdmans Books for Young Readers

Grand Rapids, Michigan

Once upon a time there was a pond,
and in that pond lived a lot of frogs.

They spent their days doing froggy
things — hopping and catching flies,
napping and playing with dragonflies.

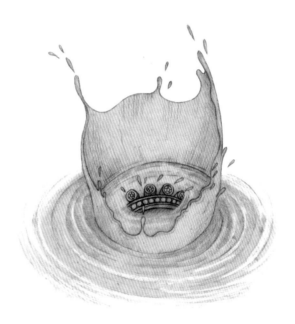

On summer nights, the frogs would sing
together after dinner. One evening while
they were singing — *groak, grak, groak* —
something fell from the sky with a PLOP!
into the water.

The frogs hurried to search the bottom
of the pond. One of the frogs had seen
the exact spot where the thing went PLOP!
and found it right away.

It was small and shiny.

It was a crown.

Crowns are for kings and queens, of course. So when they saw the frog with the crown on her head, the others said, "Look! She's the queen of the frogs!"

No one had ever seen a queen, and no one knew what to do or say. Finally one of the frogs shouted, "Long live the queen!" and clapped her hands.

"Long live the queen!" the other frogs cried, and a roar of applause rose from the pond.

But what exactly does a queen do? The frog with the crown didn't know.

A few frogs thought they knew, and gave her advice: "The queen cannot speak to the other frogs. She may not get her feet wet. She gets the biggest lily pad all to herself. The queen mustn't overdo it. She needs to sleep a lot . . . eat flies . . . give orders . . . and punish the frogs who don't obey."

So that's exactly what happened.

The queen stopped talking to the other frogs. She never got her feet wet. She demanded a giant lily pad to sit on and the fattest flies for lunch. Since she mustn't overdo it, she made the other frogs catch flies for her and her advisors, whom she kept very busy.

Some of the frogs complained: "You caught your own flies before. Why do we have to catch them for you now?"

"Because if you don't," said an advisor, "the queen will punish you."

Many things changed at the pond. The queen and
her advisors were always hungry, and the other
frogs had to catch so many flies that they were too
tired to sing at night.

One day, a frog dared to ask, "Why are you the only one who can be queen?"

"Because she found the crown," said an advisor.

"But why does that make her queen?"

"Because she was the fastest at finding it, and that means she's the queen. The queen is always the fastest and best at everything," said the advisor.

Days passed. The advisors organized a diving
tournament at the pond to entertain the queen.
"Queens love diving," said one of the advisors.
And the dives began! There were forward dives
and backward dives, upside-down dives and
twisting dives. The queen had a wonderful time!

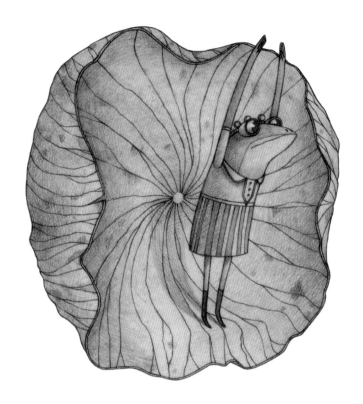

When the tournament was about to end, one of the frogs said, "Now it's your turn, dear queen."

"My turn for what?"

"The final dive, my queen. Look — we left the tallest leaf just for you."

"How dare you ask her to jump?" said an advisor.

"Because you said that she's the best at everything," said the frog. "We're waiting for her magnificent plunge into the water."

The queen knew she couldn't refuse. The leaf's height frightened her, but she climbed up and prepared to jump.

The queen counted, "One, two, three . . . "
SPLASH!
She dove deep, very deep.

When she returned to the surface, she asked,
"How did I do? Was it the best dive ever?"

But the pond was silent. Everyone stared at her.
Finally one frog said, "Where's the crown? She
doesn't have her crown anymore!"

The queen had lost her crown in the water.

"Find it!" she cried.

But the frogs said, "Who are you to order us around?"

"I am your queen!"

"You don't have a crown! You can't be queen!"

And the frogs started to throw mud balls at her.

The frogs only stopped when someone arrived at the pond in a boat. They had to hide because men in boats often caught frogs to fry and eat for dinner.

But this time, the man didn't catch a single frog. He reached into the water and stirred up the stones at the bottom of the pond. And when he pulled his hand out, he held a small, shiny object between his fingers.

It was the queen's crown!

Once upon a time, there was — and still is — a pond. And in that pond there are still a lot of frogs. But now everything has returned to normal. Queens no longer exist there, and all the frogs catch their own flies. On summer nights they sing their favorite song together, the one that goes *groak, grak, groak.*

Sometimes, up on the bridge, a pair of lovers
appears. Once, on that same bridge, the couple
argued, but now all is well.

He kisses her behind the ears. On her finger she
wears a ring that looks like a small, shiny crown.
When he kisses her, she smiles and smiles.

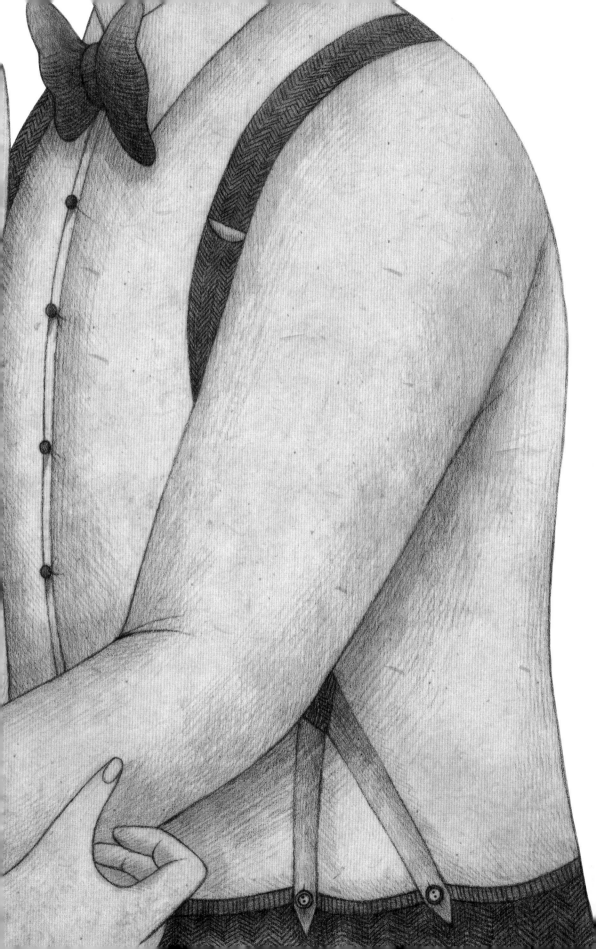

Davide Cali began his career writing comics, and his first children's book was published in 2000. Since then, he has published dozens of picture books in Italian, French, English, Portuguese, German, and Spanish, and many of those have been translated into other languages. Cali has won numerous awards, including a Special Mention at the Bologna Book Fair. He currently lives in Italy.

Marco Somà studied painting at the Academy of Fine Arts in Cuneo, Italy, and is now a professor of illustration there. Somà's illustrations have been selected for exhibitions at the Bologna Book Fair and at the Biennial in Bratislava, Slovakia. In 2015 he received the Emanuele Luzzati Prize for his illustration of the Italian edition of *The Queen of the Frogs* and two other picture books.

First published in the United States in 2017 by
Eerdmans Books for Young Readers,
an imprint of Wm. B. Eerdmans Publishing Co.
2140 Oak Industrial Dr. NE
Grand Rapids, MI 49505
www.eerdmans.com

Originally published in Portugal in 2012 by Bruaá Editora
Original title: *A rainha das rãs não pode molhar os pés*
© Bruaá Editora, 2012
Text © Davide Cali
Illustrations © Marco Somà
This edition © 2017 Eerdmans Books for Young Readers
English translation © 2017 Lyn Miller-Lachmann

Manufactured at Tien Wah Press in Malaysia

22 21 20 19 18 17   7 6 5 4 3 2 1

ISBN 978-0-8028-5481-0

A catalog listing is available from the Library of Congress.

The display type was set in Amatic SC.
The text type was set in Bookman Old Style.

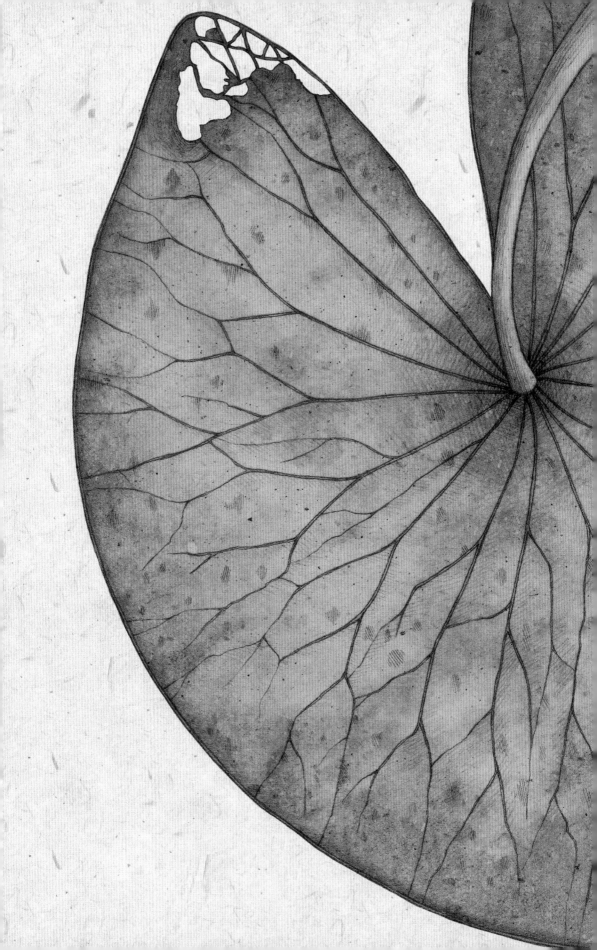